The Radiant

Shirley Lauro

A Samuel French Acting Edition

SAMUEL
FRENCH

FOUNDED 1830

SAMUELFRENCH.COM
SAMUELFRENCH-LONDON.CO.UK

FOR PRODUCTION ENQUIRIES

UNITED STATES AND CANADA
Info@SamuelFrench.com
1-866-598-8449

UNITED KINGDOM AND EUROPE
Plays@SamuelFrench-London.co.uk
020-7255-4302

Each title is subject to availability from Samuel French, depending
upon country of performance. Please be aware that THE RADIANT may
not be licensed by Samuel French in your territory. Professional and
amateur producers should contact the nearest Samuel French office or
licensing partner to verify availability.

MUSIC USE NOTE

Licensees are solely responsible for obtaining formal written permission from copyright owners to use copyrighted music in the performance of this play and are strongly cautioned to do so. If no such permission is obtained by the licensee, then the licensee must use only original music that the licensee owns and controls. Licensees are solely responsible and liable for all music clearances and shall indemnify the copyright owners of the play(s) and their licensing agent, Samuel French, against any costs, expenses, losses and liabilities arising from the use of music by licensees. Please contact the appropriate music licensing authority in your territory for the rights to any incidental music.

IMPORTANT BILLING AND CREDIT REQUIREMENTS

If you have obtained performance rights to this title, please refer to your licensing agreement for important billing and credit requirements.

THE RADIANT had its world premiere at The New Theatre in Miami, Florida, with Artistic Director, R.J. Martinez, and Managing Director, Eileen Suarez, on May 25, 2011. The production was directed by R.J. Martinez, with scenic design by Rob Eastman-Mullins, costumes by K. Blair Brown, sound by Ozzie Quintana, and lights by R.J. Martinez. The cast was as follows:

MARIE CURIE . . . . Angelica Page

KATARINA . . . . Hana Kalinski

PAUL . . . . Richard-John Seikaly, II

PAYMASTER, PROFESSOR WILBOIS, LORD KELVIN . . . . Stephen S. Neal

THE RADIANT had its New York premiere at The Red Fern Theatre, with Artistic Director, Melanie Moyer Williams, on February 21, 2013. The production was directed by Melanie Moyer Williams, with scenic design by Rowan Doyle, costumes by T. Michael Hall, and lights by Sam Gordon. The cast was as follows:

MARIE CURIE . . . . Diana LaMar

KATARINA . . . . Rachel Berger

PAUL . . . . A.J. Cedano

PAYMASTER, PROFESSOR WILBOIS, LORD KELVIN . . . . . Timothy Doyle

CHARACTERS

MARIE SKLODOWSKA CURIE – Polish, but in France many years. Late 30s-to-mid-40s. Ethereal beauty – ash blond, small, graceful, piercing eyes, intense manner reveals brilliance of a genius. A unique, complex woman of great strength, drive. Can be severe, steely. "Suffers no fools gladly". Hides extreme shyness, high emotionality behind exterior demeanor. Dresses in black clothes of period. Straw summer hat, light colored blouse in country and light colored blouse through Act II. Has cough, possibly some nervous mannerisms.

KATARINA – 17. Marie's niece from Warsaw. Pretty, funny, strong spirited but not contemporary teen – rather of era when young people ruled by adults. Loveable, impulsive, dramatic, but tries to contain herself. Clothing: blouse with possible touch of Polish style embroidery, dark longish skirt of period. In Normandy, light summery blouse, straw hat with flowers.

PAUL LANGEVIN – early 30's. Handsome, youthful, French. Brilliant but naïve, sensual man. Repressed, yearns to break out. White shirt, vest, student type jacket. Later in dark suit/trousers.

*CHIEF PAYMASTER OF THE SORBONNE – Middle-age. Epitome of bureaucrat, a lecher. Possible pince-nez, vest, time-piece in vest. French accent.

*PROFESSOR WILBOIS – Late middle-age. Physics professor at Sorbonne. Kindly, loveable. Somewhat absent minded–maybe a stain or two on clothing, missing button on vest, etc. From Alsace-Lorraine, possibly has slight French/German accent.

*LORD KELVIN – Middle-aged. Physics Professor, University of Edinburgh. A Scotsman (either Scottish or English accent.). Possibly reddish hair. Pompous, blustery, condescending. Possibly smokes pipe; possibly in clothing with Scotch plaid/argyle design touches. Elegant in appearance.

* (Characters designed to be portrayed by one actor. Concept: for Marie they are the outside world: men of power surrounding her, with whom she must relate and/or struggle. Chief Paymaster and Kelvin are in opposition to her. Wilbois, sympathetic, but forced to bear bad news.)

PLACE

Paris, Normandy, Provence, France; and Stockholm, Sweden
The play is performed without Intermission.

TIME

Over a hundred years ago.

PLAYWRIGHT'S SUGGESTIONS FOR PRODUCTION VALUES

The Radiant has been inspired by the life of Marie Curie. The events told of her life in the play are true. To help tell her story, I have enhanced and/or created some characters .

The play is the psychological journey of Marie Curie from penniless widow with two children to her final victory in isolating radium and the consequences of that. It is Marie's singular journey, and all directorial and design elements should be guided by that.

SET

The play is driven by the complex, unique character of Marie. So – ideally, set not realistic but a cinematic space or landscape which is fluid and can easily become several different locations for her as she psychologically moves through time and place in her journey in the play. A unit set. No lumbering scenery, metal tracks, welding, turntables, or other devices. Few pieces of furniture moved around for various scenes, minimal props. Unit set used denoting parts of each room – such as, for Parlor on unit: section of room with two small chairs, and between chairs, small table (that could hold tea service, possible teacart) – all of the period. A samovar. No doors, actors step from space to space on unit set which should have steps, levels, etc. Full descriptions are given for each change of scene. These are to help designers find essence of the scene – the part to show audience. Not meant to be realistically manifest on stage. The full description is also for cast and other designers to get the feel of exactly where the characters are.

LIGHTS

Heavy emphasis on lighting. Beautiful and strategic in creating shifting scenes of time and place – and the moods of Marie as she moves through play. The CROSS FADES of the lights carry the continuous shifting of places and times. Blackouts used sparingly if at all.

COSTUMES

Apt, striking clothing of era. Costumes both signaling and emblematic of time and characters. But play not overburdened with costumes.
Designer(s) who can design poetically.

To: Lou, Andrea, Joshua, and Melanie

(Paris, 1906)

(Lights up: The Sorbonne, Paris. Accounting Office)

(CHIEF PAYMASTER *on high stool, writing.* **MARIE,** *in black cape, enters, waiting for him to look up. He does not.)*

MARIE. I am Madame Curie. I believe we had an appointment, monsieur?

PAYMASTER. *Oui...?*

(looks at her bewildered)

An <u>appointment</u>?

(looks through some scattered, messy schedule books, finding it)

Ah – so we do! But as you can understand – I have so many appointments? You of course must be Professor Pierre Curie's widow?

(Smiles artificially, subtly looking her over in a sexual way. She shifts stance away from him.)

How sorry I am, personally, Madame – since I've heard – here at our Sorbonne – Pierre Curie's Nobel Prize brought honor to *all of France*!

MARIE. I've come to discuss receiving my husband's salary for the term.

PAYMASTER. But of course –

(Goes back to stool, sits, searching for other papers which He can't find. **MARIE** *watches, impatient.)*

MARIE. Perhaps I should come another time?

PAYMASTER. Uh – No – Ah! "Pierre Curie" – but *so long ago* – there may be a Statute of Limitations – no – *however* – his sudden and untimely death occurred before the seminars ended. What a pity it happened *before* – rather than *after.*

MARIE. There were only three sessions left to teach, Monsieur.

PAYMASTER. Nonetheless: "Deceased employee shall have completed *entire* work period for survivor to receive deceased's salary." But his seminars ended abruptly, unfortunately. – no faculty member capable of completing the course? Sessions <u>abandoned</u> – Students required to take <u>deferments</u>. Impossible to request *any* kind of salary, Madame. Which – of course – I would very much like to do –

(She glares at him, steps back. He busies himself, thumbing through folder, stops, pulls out envelope, rips open, to read.)

MARIE. *(Interrupting)* Please! Let me not detain you any longer, Monsieur – ?

(She starts out.)

PAYMASTER. Ah hah! Here's something *very* much in your favor! What luck we are in!

(She stops.)

MARIE. *We* are in luck?

PAYMASTER. You are entitled to: <u>"The Widow's Pension"</u>! Ah, la, la!

MARIE. *(shocked)* "Pension"?

PAYMASTER. "To continue until: 1.) widow's demise – 2.) remarriage – 3.) through all lingering illnesses. But – should widow obtain work of any nature? All benefits <u>cease</u>!"

MARIE. I can't *work*? I am educated –

(He pulls check from envelope.)

PAYMASTER. Your initial check! 54% of husband's salary. Every <u>month</u>! Now – we'll add your name – "Marie" – your full name, please?

MARIE. Marie Salomea Sklodowska Curie –

(He shoots her a suspicious but subtle look.)

PAYMASTER. Salomea – Old Testament name, yes?

MARIE. Yes –

PAYMASTER. And Sklowdowska – Southern Russia?

MARIE. *(annoyed)* Polish!

PAYMASTER. But of course. So – what a happy ending we have here. And – should there be any problems – contact me? Once you are on the books, make another appointment? For a larger pension – perhaps? *Under certain privileged circumstances* – I may devise a way!

(Puts check in her hand, sliding other hand slowly up her arm while holding her hand with check. **MARIE** *breaks away abruptly; disgusted, afraid.)*

MARIE. Monsieur! Please!

PAYMASTER. Only the best intentions, Madame – the very best –

(She looks at check.)

MARIE. You have misspelled "Sklodowska", Monsieur Paymaster! And your arithmetic as to what my "Widow's Pension" was to be? Incorrect!

(She rips check, throws on floor, storms from room.)

(Cross fade as we follow **MARIE** *down hallway to enter* **PIERRE**'*s office. Desk, papers still there. 2 chairs, some books, diplomas on wall.)*

*(***PAUL** *sits on floor stacking books in box.* **MARIE** *is surprised to see him.)*

MARIE. Paul!

PAUL. Madame! I'm packing up the rest of Pierre's things – I'll send them to you –

MARIE. I – I wanted to see the office one more time, Paul. I – I had other business here besides – "The – the – Chief Paymaster" –

PAUL. "Paymaster"?

MARIE. Trivial…except I learned from him Pierre's seminar in "Radioactivity" is being abandoned!

PAUL. No!

MARIE. God knows the ramifications of that.

(She looks around.)

All the same still –

(awkward pause)

(He is taken aback at her thin appearance, hides this, goes to her quickly, kissing her hand.)

PAUL. Your cape, Madame?

(He makes gesture to help her but she keeps it protectively wraps it around herself, looking around Pierre's office.)

(an awkward pause)

MARIE. It's been a long time, yes?

(She's very affected by this, turns away from him.)

(another awkward pause)

PAUL. Pierre's funeral? Not so long, is it?

MARIE. Time is relative, Paul –

(She smiles. He smiles back.)

(another awkward silence)

PAUL. You – you're looking well, Madame. Fashionably thin –

MARIE. *(sardonically, laughing a little)* Madame Curie? *Haute couture? Oo, la, la!*

(She chuckles.)

(pause)

I don't look well at all.

(They are connecting. He smiles gently at her as she admires him.)

But – you? The very picture of youth – health!

(beat)

PAUL. Truthfully –

(He turns away.)

I'm exhausted, Madame. Teaching general science – three lower girls' schools –

MARIE. *(shocked)* Not working on your doctorate, or even –

PAUL. *(cutting in)* I – I dropped out.

(awkward silence)

(He moves away, guilty, aware of her eyes on him.)

Clotilde's had our third child – her mother's with us – I *have* to earn a good salary, Madame –

MARIE. Three children? A wife? A mother-in-law? Six mouths to feed on part-time salaries from lower schools? *Your wife's* willing to live on that?

(He turns to her.)

PAUL. No, she wants me rich in her family publishing business.

(silence)

MARIE. *(Upset, searching his eyes)* You were Pierre's protégé! My prize lab student! In our home – dinner – wine by the fire discussing science – I was so invested in you – Paul – still –

(silence)

PAUL. A long time ago, Madame –

(He starts packing books from open box on floor.)

MARIE. Yes –

(moments pass)

But – as we said – time is relative –

(pause)

There's no work at the lab, you know.

PAUL. Weren't you doing an important experiment with Pierre?

MARIE. I couldn't bear going there alone! I ran out terrified!

PAUL. *(surprised)* But Marcel was –

MARIE. I can afford him only a few hours –

(*She lowers her head.*)

We were living on Pierre's salary.

(*long silence*)

(*near tears*)

Paul – I – I – need a job – I'd be willing to travel to the suburbs…you…you know of anything?

PAUL. A *general school science teacher*? *You* just berated *me* for that.

(*She turns away. He gives her his hanky. She clutches hanky, looks at him.*)

MARIE. There's nothing else I'm trained to do –

(*Several beats, then she absently picks up notebook from* **PIERRE**'s *desk.*)

Pierre's last notes?

(*She scans through notebook.*)

He – he forgot something here –

(*She takes pen from* **PIERRE**'s *desk, starts making notations in the notebook.*)

And this is not correct!

(*She scratches something out.*)

(*beat*)

(**PAUL** *moves away, then turns, scrutinizing her.*)

PAUL. Madame? Pierre's Chair at the Sorbonne is empty –

MARIE. *(a little laugh)*

Of course it's empty: he's dead!

PAUL. That's not what I meant.

MARIE. What then?

PAUL. When a head faculty member dies – his closest colleague inherits his Chair – that's the tradition…

(She stops writing abruptly looking at him, rising.)

MARIE. What are you getting at?

(beat)

PAUL. That you could be appointed to Pierre's Chair –

(beat)

MARIE. I never want to set foot in here after today!

PAUL. No one will ever teach "Radioactivity" then. You're the only one equipped – the discovery will slide to someone else's hands –

(She looks back at him.)

MARIE. They would never let me teach here!

PAUL. But you got the first doctorate a woman's ever been given and you *discovered the field*!

MARIE. Me? His "Little Assistant Wife"? I wasn't *mentioned* at the Nobel! My name wasn't even on our Prize until Pierre insisted.

PAUL. I didn't know that.

MARIE. You're a Frenchman. You don't know that French men see women only "on the street" or "in their husbands' beds"?

(She turns away.)

(silence)

(She begins thumbing through books.)

Pierre *always* honored that it was my discovery. But he's gone –

PAUL. You've got to go on alone Madame! Go on! Sit! It's yours!

(He holds out chair for her. she looks at him quickly then turns away, pacing, thinking. Moments pass. She stops.)

(She looks around room once more, then sits in **PIERRE**'*s chair.)*

(Silence. Then she picks up pen, takes out paper.)

MARIE. Oscar Wilbois – he heads the Committee on Faculty Appointments – yes?

PAUL. I – I think so –

(Beat. **MARIE** *begins writing.)*

MARIE. I'm writing him to put me forward –

(She keeps writing, then looks up at him a moment.)

If I were to be appointed – would – would there be any chance y*ou – you* possibly could help me –

PAUL. *Me?*

MARIE. You were his protégé, after all –

PAUL. I – I don't –

MARIE. *(interrupting)* I'll be earning a good salary. I could give you a stipend. Large grants – research fellowships are emerging all over in science, Paul – maybe I could get you one –

PAUL. "I have six mouths to feed" – as you put it.

(silence)

(She gets up, walks around.)

MARIE. You know – Pierre and I were hoping to start a co-operative school – professors teaching each other's children in each other's homes. *Maybe* – besides a Fellowship I could get you a *special honorarium* to help me with a school like that. Certainly you could drop teaching those lower girls' schools then?

(silence)

*(***PAUL** *thinks this over.)*

PAUL. The whole thing is quite a gamble!

(They look at each other, smile. A moment of deep connection passing between them.)

(beat)

MARIE. If I weren't a gambler, Paul – I'd still be a tutor in the Polish countryside!

(She shakes his hand.)

For gambler's luck, stack all those books back as they were, please?

(They both smile.)

Oh – first – put this in Wilbois' box for me?

(She hands him note)

PAUL. Of course.

MARIE. I think I'll stay here awhile…alone…

(He starts out. She pulls something from pocket.)

Your hanky.

(He turns back. She offers it.)

PAUL. Keep it – for gambler's luck – "Marie" –

*(She connects with him as he calls her "**MARIE**." He exits. She looks after him, holding hanky to her cheek a moment.)*

(Cross fade to parlor in **MARIE***'s home. Later. Period chairs, small table between them, teacart or side board.)*

*(***KATARINA*** enters with tea tray. Pours tea from shiny Polish samovar on sideboard.* **PAUL** *enters.)*

PAUL. *Bonjour,* Mademoiselle – I'm Paul Langevin.

KATARINA. *Bonjour,* Monsieur.

PAUL. But – didn't we meet at your uncle's funeral? – part of Madame's family? From Warsaw?

KATARINA. Her niece – Katarina.

PAUL. You stayed on?

KATARINA. *(strikes a slightly dramatic pose)* No, the family decided I was the one to come back – help Aunt Marie get back on her feet – she's been in such deep mourning – and, of course – what could I do but volunteer myself?

(He gives her bouquet of roses.)

Oh – she dearly loves roses! I'll arrange them – in a crystal vase on the tea tray. Here, monsieur – the parlor? I'll tell Aunt Marie you're here –

(She exits. Moment as **PAUL** *looks around.* **MARIE** *enters.)*

MARIE. Paul!

PAUL. Soon as I heard, I came.

MARIE. *(imitating, with German accent)* "We invite you <u>to join the faculty</u>!"

(She laughs.)

Wilbois came personally last night.

PAUL. I'm thrilled, Marie!

*(***KATARINA*** stops at doorway, a moment, listening. Hearing* **PAUL** *say "Marie", she bumps against door.)*

MARIE. Katarina?

KATARINA. I was arranging the roses.

(KATARINA enters, setting down vase of flowers, arranging dishes, etc.)

They're from Monsieur.

(She covertly looks from one to the other.)

MARIE. Roses!

PAUL. I – I remembered you used to always have them –

(He smiles at MARIE. KATARINA serves them.)

KATARINA. Maybe you can persuade Aunt Marie to try a pastry today?

PAUL. Persuade?

KATARINA. Well –

(She glances at MARIE, then bursts into story with a theatrical flair.)

She's not eating! Can't hold anything down! – and she has a cough! It all just simply scares me to DEATH! What she needs is a new <u>doctor</u> and –

MARIE. *(interrupting)* Katarina? Maybe you'd enjoy taking the children to the park?

KATARINA. *(deflated)* What? Oh – of course –

(PAUL drinks, eats, notices MARIE doesn't.)

PAUL. That's why you're so thin?

(KATARINA exits, stays outside listening.)

MARIE. Katarina is just turning seventeen. And is very dramatic.

(PAUL chuckles. KATARINA, hearing her name, stops, moves closer again to listen at door.)

PAUL. You won't take a bite of the pastry?

MARIE. I barely eat. Mourning Pierre is taking its toll. But Katarina wants me fat and jolly now – so she can go home to Warsaw.

PAUL. Misses her family?

MARIE. Her beau, Stefan! They plan to start at the conservatory this fall together – become "concert pianists"! She tells me they will play on the same stage at the same time – on <u>twin</u> pianos! God help us!

(She chuckles as does **PAUL.** **KATARINA**, *listening, bumps against door again.)*

Katarina? I thought you were taking the children to the park?

KATARINA. Uh – they're playing with the cat, upstairs. Would you like more tea?

MARIE. No thank you, Katarina.

*(***KATARINA*** exits.)*

PAUL. Well – only stopped by to congratulate you – I'll be leaving – I think there's some sort of protocol book about inaugural lectures for new professors. I'll make inquiries to the department. Good-night – Madame – Mademoiselle –

(He exits. **KATARINA** *enters.)*

MARIE. Katya? Don't develop the miserable habit of listening in doorways or overdramatize to Paul – about me or my affairs or –

KATARINA. *(bewildered)* "Overdramatize"?

MARIE. Saying I won't eat – can't hold down food! Nothing of my personal life is to be revealed to anyone! Please!

(silence)

KATARINA. But Paul's an old friend – coming back to the lab –

MARIE. He'll be teaching at the Sorbonne only. I've suspended operations in the lab.

(pause)

KATARINA. Well – I'm glad!

MARIE. Why on earth would –

KATARINA. *(cutting in, mysteriously)* Something is very wrong in there!

MARIE. Wrong?

KATARINA. That day you sent me for your notebooks? Marcel said – the very minute I came in –

(impulsively and very dramatically, as Marcel:)

"Katarina, look! All nine guinea pigs died! <u>Overnight</u>!" And there they all were in the cage, Aunt Manya.

(She starts seeing them now, imitating their pose with her hands up.)

Stiff! Legs up! Oh my God!

MARIE. *(nonplussed)* Guinea pigs die in labs every day, Katya. Shall we end this ridiculous discussion now? And please don't swear in my presence?

*(***KATARINA*** picks up tray to exit.)*

Oh – don't go – there's something I do want to discuss with you.

KATARINA. Yes?

MARIE. I've just been appointed to your Uncle Pierre's position at the Sorbonne for fall.

KATARINA. *(ecstatic)* But that's wonderful for you!

(She runs and embraces her.)

MARIE. It will mean a good salary, Katya –

*(***MARIE*** leads ***KATARINA*** to sit, as does ***MARIE***.)*

But I need to start preparing now! Quite hard! Lectures to organize – papers to read – articles – faculty meetings – and an Inaugural Lecture to give –

(beat)

*(She takes both ***KATARINA***'s hands.)*

I – I know this will be hard for you – and a surprise – but the children love you so – and I love and trust you so with them – I – I need you to stay on – help me? You can go home January – February – you can leave then –

(silence)

KATARINA. August is what we agreed on, Aunt Manya – so I could find a tutoring job…

MARIE. It's a critical step for me…I'll make it up to you – a salary by fall you can save for school – and I – I'll try very hard to arrange a holiday for you to see Stefan –

KATARINA. Stefan and I are entering the conservatory *together* September first!

MARIE. The conservatory won't run away!

KATARINA. But we're taking a duet piano practicum! What – what if he takes it with someone else?

(She starts imagining this horror.)

Like <u>Raissa</u>?

MARIE. Will you grow up? Don't you see how little anyone's life turns out the way they planned – or hoped – or dreamed?

KATARINA. You promised!!

MARIE. Write your mother at once! Tell her I'm taking your Uncle Pierre's Chair at the Sorbonne and must ask that you stay until after the New Year!

*(**MARIE** exits.)*

(Cross fade to same Parlor, two weeks later.)

*(**PAUL** enters from outside, **MARIE** from house.)*

PAUL. Madame? Madame? I found the protocol book.

(He pulls book from briefcase.)

"Introduction for Acceptance of Professorship".

(He thumbs through book.)

Here: "At inaugural lecture, incoming professor commences with 1.) a salute of gratitude to Ministers of Education, University Officers, and Council of the Faculty of Science, designating all."

(He looks at her.)

MARIE. But – "The Ministers of Education"? They're the ones that offered me that cursed pension, aren't they? And nearly half the science faculty council were against me in the end! Now I'm supposed to give them a "salute of gratitude"? Besides – I'm paralyzed at *the thought* of Public Speaking!

PAUL. You have to play the game, Marie.

(She glares at him.)

MARIE. You still have no idea how impossible this is for me?

PAUL. *(reading)*

"I wish to express my deep gratitude to The Ministers of Education"

(He is writing words on piece of paper.)

– Then we name them – they'll be front row.

(writing)

Secondly, you will give – Here –

(Holds out paper to her. She only looks at him.)

Marie? You said you needed help!

(She takes paper, stumbling.)

MARIE. "And – I wish to express my – deep – grat – gratitude – to the – Council of the Faculty – of Science – for granting me the – the – priv – priv –

(She crumples paper, glaring at him.)

PAUL. You've got the position – this is all just *pro forma.*

MARIE. I *can't* do it!

(She turns away. He consults book again.)

PAUL. We'll work on that later then. "2.) Eulogy to your predecessor". Let me –

MARIE. *(interrupting)* Are you insane? You imagine I can stand up in public and provide an afternoon's entertainment for the faculty, press, and Parisian Society by speaking about my extraordinary husband who died a monstrous death?

(She's close to tears.)

PAUL. But the tradition is –

MARIE. *(interrupting)* *"Tradition?"* You think that has anything to do with me? You understand nothing about me! NOTHING!

(She grabs Protocol Book from him and throws it to floor. Silence.)

PAUL. *(softly)* How *can I* help you then?

(silence)

MARIE. It has to be my way. There can be no other way.

(Beat. Then starting out.)

God! I've gotten a miserable headache, Paul…another time…?

*(Scene shifts: two months later. Same Parlor. **KATARINA**, entering Parlor with brooch, calling:)*

KATARINA. Auntie Manya? Auntie Manya?

*(**MARIE** enters.)*

Wear Grandmother's brooch? I brought it just for you.

*(**MARIE** looks, gives it back.)*

MARIE. I'll wear it Christmas.

KATARINA. But the Fall Inaugural Lecture at the Sorbonne is a *very* special occasion!

*(She stops short. **MARIE** looking at her, frightened.)*

MARIE. Please! Don't dress me up! Help me pretend it's just an ordinary day of teaching! It's the only way I have a hope of getting through this.

(Lights up on Sorbonne Auditorium. Later.)

*(**MARIE** comes to podium to address audience. **KATARINA** and **PAUL** stand in wings.)*

I wish to express my – dee – deep –

(She begins to cough, clears throat, grasps podium, breathes with difficulty.)

I – I wish to express –

*(She glances at **PAUL**, crumples first page of lecture, goes to her own notes.)*

Let me begin – begin today by say – saying this seminar will continue in the exact place where Professor Pierre Curie left off. But – for this inaugural session? A short review!

*(She glances at **PAUL** again, gaining confidence, then looking at audience, directly.)*

At first, Professor Curie and I believed the rays' energy from the uranium atoms was coming from the sun. Scientist Lord Kelvin, University of Glasgow, was the prime proponent of the "sun theory".

But then? We discovered the uranium atom, left in the dark in a drawer with no sun at all was still emitting high energy rays!

(She steps closer and closer to audience, more informal, intimate, speaking directly to them.)

Next, we found that the energy rays from the uranium atom were coming, not from the sun, but from inside the uranium atom's nucleus itself. These energy rays didn't depend on any external factors at all – light of the sun, temperature, rain, snow – nothing!

Instead, we found that energy rays were always found in association with the uranium atom!

(Still closer, beginning to talk to audience individually.)

Therefore, smaller components inside the uranium atom *could* exist. And the components could be active – emitting rays. In actuality one of these components was capable of emitting intense energy rays. I named the component "radium". And I called the process "radioactivity."

(*She moves back behind science table, puts notes away, takes off glasses.*)

MARIE. (*cont.*) That ends today's lecture. Next week, I will speak on radioactive substances.

(*She bows slightly to applause.* **PAUL** *and* **KATARINA** *rush to her. She is suddenly pale, trembling, close to fainting. She recuperates a bit.*)

PAUL. You were extraordinary!

KATARINA. I was so proud!

(**MARIE** *turns to* **PAUL.**)

MARIE. My *throat* was in spasm – my *hands* trembling! Paul, you should have made me practice more.

PAUL. (*chuckling*) *Me?* I could barely get in the room with you! Besides – no one noticed anything except your triumph! All of Paris! And they were enthralled – and still as mice.

MARIE. (*laughing lightly*) With the mentality of mice, most of them –

(*He gives her flowers.*)

Thank you, Paul – they're lovely –

KATARINA. (*excited*) We've planned a champagne toast for you now, in the lab garden – with a coconut almond cake!

(*She exits.*)

MARIE. I couldn't begin to swallow rich cake – or drink champagne –

PAUL. At least come to the lab garden with us?

(**MARIE** *looks at* **PAUL** *quickly.*)

MARIE. The lab is closed!

(*beat*)

(**MARIE** *breaks away, starting off.*)

PAUL. Where are you going?

MARIE. To Pierre!

PAUL. What?

KATARINA. Aunt Marie?

(Silence. **MARIE** *is gone.)*

PAUL. *(calling after her)* Wait – wait –

(Cross fade: **PIERRE**'s *gravestone, cemetery. Later.)*

*(***MARIE** *enters, crosses to grave, carrying bouquet. She kneels, putting flowers on grave one at a time, then, listening, senses another presence. Looking around.)*

MARIE. *(whispering)* Pierre? You're here! I – I just did the inaugural lecture for your class – stumbled – coughed – but I did it! Are you proud of me?

(She adds a flower.)

They've given me your office. And I'll hate being there – but I know I must accept that. And everything else. Remember how we promised each other we'd go on with the work if the other were gone? I took that first step! God, it's so impossibly hard! Do you know what I really want? To run away to the country with the girls – be a real mother – ride bicycles with them – chase fireflies – make gooseberry jam and bread together – then sit alone by the fire at night and rest – but I can't!

(beat)

Stay close? Watch over the children – me? My birthday's tomorrow! Help me through –

*(***PAUL** *enters quietly, behind her. She senses him.)*

(beat)

PAUL. Come to Pierre's office with me? Science department's deserted – they just put your name on the door.

(She looks away.)

Start making it yours – walk around – look at the view – plan what you want on the walls –

MARIE. *Somewhere* there must be another empty office!

PAUL. It's an honor, Marie –

MARIE. It's cruel! *He's not there!*

(She turns from him to grave, laying more flowers.)

(A long silence. She's beginning to cry. then, whispering:)

When I put my head on his coffin lid before they lowered him…his energy came right through to me. And now before you came? I felt it again. We were agnostics…but we believed there was only a thin veil between the living and the dead – their energy flows back and forth to us…you see, we believed in that kind of energy too. My big sister died when I was eight – my mother – when I was ten –

PAUL. *(whispering)* Yes?

MARIE. The only comfort I found? Not God – but pretending I was a doctor – who went to the moon and discovered the magic cure to bring them back to life – I felt my sister and mother's energy around me then – and I promised them over and over that's what I would do – when I grew up I would find the magic cure –

(Silence. Then whispering, sobbing, fighting hysteria.)

His head was crushed by horses' hooves…he'd slipped on the street – horses pulling a wagon – loaded with military uniforms – my great pacifist husband –

PAUL. Shh! I know –

MARIE. *(more hysterical)* His magnificent brain – splattered all over the Paris Boulevard –

(He pulls her up, as she cries, embraces her tightly. She buries her head in his chest blurting out in a daze of pain.)

Junks of it stuck on his overcoat – I tore it – burned it in the fireplace…shred by shred by shred –

(He kisses her and they stay in embrace. Finally she quietens.)

PAUL. It's starting to rain.

(He puts his jacket around her.)

It's macabre here! Let's go –

(He puts arm around her. She puts her head on his shoulder. They exit.)

(Cross fade. Two months later. **MARIE**'s *office.)*

(She's on a chair, stacking books on a shelf, doesn't see **LORD KELVIN** *enters.)*

KELVIN. Well – Madame Curie…

(She whirls around.)

MARIE. Yes?

KELVIN. Lord Kelvin, Madame!

MARIE. *(surprised, then smiling)* Lord Kelvin? We've met – but years ago, wasn't it?

(He kisses her hand.)

KELVIN. Only now – your name's on the door, Madame! Something of a shock – but very impressive indeed!

MARIE. Thank you, Lord Kelvin –

(He walks around.)

KELVIN. Well – all of his books still intact on the shelves – far as I can tell – you've left all the ones of significance, I dare say?

MARIE. All of them are there.

(He looks around walls.)

KELVIN. But his diplomas – citations? Plaques?

MARIE. My daughter, Irène, has put them up in her room –

KELVIN. Appropriate, appropriate to be sure!

(He's reading **MARIE**'s *diplomas on wall.)*

Then too – it lets us all enjoy yours here, Madame.

(She looks at him.)

KELVIN. *(cont.)* His name's on your diploma, here – you were Pierre's student straight the way through I imagine – many, many years his junior – 10 – 15 years?

(She nods.)

What a fine teacher he must have been…along with his magnificent research on rad –

MARIE. *(interrupting)* I began the research on radium. He followed my lead.

(He looks at children's photos on desk.)

KELVIN. Even added the children's photos?

(He smiles at her.)

What shall I say – such a motherly touch – ?

MARIE. I am their mother, Lord Kelvin.

KELVIN. The wee one?

MARIE. Èvette?

KELVIN. Favors Pierre – either of them inherit his genius?

(beat)

MARIE. Mostly they play with the cat –

(He keeps looking around, **MARIE** *growing very wary.)*

And you, sir? What brings you to Paris? And to me?

(He sits, having not been invited to.)

KELVIN. First off, to extend condolences, Madame, on Pierre's untimely death.

MARIE. But such a long trip from the University of Glasgow to pay a condolence call? Especially since it's been so long since Pierre –

KELVIN. *(interrupting)* Other reasons, of course, bring me to Paris, Madame. I've been interviewing for a "guest lectureship" here – at a stupendous University, to say the least – St. Mary's Catholic Institute! You've heard of it, of course?

(She thinks a moment, skeptical.)

MARIE. "Guest Lectureship"? You're on Sabbatical from Glasgow then?

KELVIN. Just came from the interview at St. Mary's in fact! Went remarkably well, I must say. No decision yet, of course – but full appointment without doubt second term. A seminar on my theory of radium. I proposed it to them and they invited me over from Glasgow to discuss it.

MARIE. *Your* theory of radium?

(She looks sharply at him, as he waxes professorial, as if lecturing.)

KELVIN. "Uranium receives its energy from the external source of the sun! Not – as your Curie Theory erroneously claims from within the uranium atom because an atom is our smallest unit. So – it cannot be opened up – split!"

(She is stunned.)

Actually – I stopped by to posit something, Madame –

MARIE. What?

KELVIN. A public discussion between us on our differing theories – next term – in the spring. With both universities sponsoring the event. St. Mary's has tentatively approved – pending my appointment in –

(She is controlled, but interrupts.)

MARIE. Mine is not a *theory*, however, Lord Kelvin. It is a proven fact. Radium is element 88. Pierre and I and Becquerel won The Nobel Prize for discovering it – some years ago now – as I'm sure you remember. *Yours was* a theory, sir – that has been disproven.

(He looks at her.)

KELVIN. Science is *always* open to re-examination, however, is it not, Madame? To be sure, the best scientists in the world once believed the earth was flat!

(He takes document from pocket.)

Now – St. Mary's Curriculum Committee asked me to bring this document to you to sign and present to your Committee. A tentative agreement for the event.

(She looks at it.)

MARIE. You must be jesting with me, Lord Kelvin –

KELVIN. *(testily)* You're not going to make an issue of this are you, Madame? It will just be an evening – wonderful event for students, science faculty –

(She hands back document.)

(silence)

(She is studying him.)

MARIE. Tell me, Lord Kelvin – if Pierre and I did not discover radium – what was it you *imagined* we *did* discover?

KELVIN. Brilliant as he was – what Pierre discovered was not the new element of radium in a saline solution – but – in all probability – simply a molecular compound of helium and lead!

(She rises.)

MARIE. Molecular Compound of *Helium*? And *lead*?

KELVIN. It cannot be an element. It was never separated from its chlorine/saline solution to stand alone as metal.

MARIE. That is trivial!

KELVIN. Really?

MARIE. And I believe you know it is!

KELVIN. But – you were his "colleague" as you say – heavily involved? Highly *influential in persuading* Pierre he'd discovered the new element of radium, I daresay –

MARIE. We did joint research and independently reached the same result!

KELVIN. Pierre was already – of course – an extraordinarily esteemed scientist! Man of greatest distinction – recognized internationally – while for *you*, Madame – well, I must say – for you? Discovering a new element has been *incredibly* significant in your career! Landed you in this office, didn't it?

MARIE. I don't know what you're –

(*PAUL enters office with books.*)

PAUL. Oh – excuse me.

MARIE. My assistant, Monsieur Langevin, Lord Kelvin. If you will excuse me now, Lord Kelvin? I have work to do with Monsieur Langevin?

(*She offers back agreement document which he takes.*)

KELVIN. 'Til we meet again – *Madame* Curie –

(*He exits.*)

MARIE. You know what just happened, Paul?

PAUL. (*shrugging*) Should I?

MARIE. He's going to take the discovery away from me –

PAUL. Don't be silly!

MARIE. I have an instinct about it!

PAUL. You always have some kind of instinct about something.

(*silence*)

MARIE. The radium's still in a *saline solution* – trivial – but not to my detractors!

(*long silence*)

(*pacing, thinking*)

I've been told Georges LeBlanc died –

PAUL. LeBlanc?

MARIE. A member of the French Academy of Science. It leaves a vacancy in my division.

PAUL. (*interrupting*) *What* are you think –

MARIE. Wilbois is a member there, isn't he? He always supports me. I'll ask him to now.

PAUL. For the Academy?

MARIE. Membership would solidify my discovery! Then *nobody* could take it away from me!

(*She gathers her books and exits. He tidies the office, bewildered. She returns.*)

MARIE. My lecture's now –

(*He takes his books, following her out.*)

(*Cross fade to parlor. Five months later. Spring.*)

(**KATARINA** *is making tea in samovar as* **WILBOIS** *enters.*)

WILBOIS. Professor Wilbois, Mademoiselle?

(*He doffs hat.*)

KATARINA. Yes?

WILBOIS. I've come to see your aunt.

KATARINA. Please come in – I'll let her know you're here.

(*He steps into parlor, she takes his hat.*)

WILBOIS. You are Madame's Polish niece, yes?

(*She nods.*)

So – what could an old man say besides, "*Charmante! Charmante!*"

KATARINA. (*drinking in compliment, giggling*)

Oh, thank you! Thank you very much! Do sit down!

(*He sits, she brings him tea.*)

The tea is from a very special Polish urn in fact.

WILBOIS. Ahh! Such fragrance it makes! From Poland, no? A – a – "samavier".

KATARINA. (*giggling*) "Sam – o – var", Professor Wilbois – "Samovar."

WILBOIS. "Samovar."

KATARINA. Exactly!

WILBOIS. So. You will join me, mademoiselle?

KATARINA. (*giggling*) Oh, thank you, Monsieur –

(Enjoying this immensely, she sits in MARIE's chair, sips from MARIE's cup.)

WILBOIS. Could be you are planning following in your aunt's illustrious footsteps? Also becoming a "scientist extraordinaire"?

KATARINA. No – no – I am a musician!

WILBOIS. An artiste! Ah! And what instrument is it you play?

KATARINA. (*posing, again dramatically*) I am a concert pianist! I –

(MARIE enters. WILBOIS rises, KATARINA slides quickly from MARIE's chair.)

MARIE. Oscar! You must've come directly from the meeting!

(He kisses MARIE's hand. MARIE sits. KATARINA gathers used teacup, gets fresh one for MARIE, MARIE nods for her to leave. KATARINA exits. He drinks. MARIE watches him, not eating, not drinking, waiting for him to tell her results. He's avoiding the entire issue.)

(a very awkward pause)

WILBOIS. So – uh – everyone says what a masterful job you do with the seminar, Madame. And in such a little time –

MARIE. Shall we just say I'm trying?

(another very awkward pause)

MARIE. Oscar?

WILBOIS. Madame?

MARIE. At the meeting tonight –

WILBOIS. Such a lovely spring night – everyone comes! Filled to capacity! So – maybe I pour myself more tea? Madame?

(She shakes head "no".)

(awkward pause)

(He pours more tea.)

MARIE. About the meeting?

(He spills tea on table cloth.)

WILBOIS. *(still avoiding issue) Ach*! I've spilt the tea, Madame!
On your lace tablecloth! I'll just wipe it off.

(He begins wiping cloth with his napkin.)

MARIE. I've not been accepted.

(silence)

Édouard Branly won my seat.

(WILBOIS *nods, continues wiping.)*

(silence)

WILBOIS. He is 72, Madame. Won by only two votes. You
will have your turn later.

MARIE. Vacancies occur very seldom, yes?

(beat)

WILBOIS. He was a senior scientist – and the Academy felt –
he was entitled now. That is all there is to say, Madame.
Please?

(beat)

MARIE. There's more than his age to this, Oscar, isn't there?
His work was minor – a wireless conductor he invented
– for *Marconi's* radio – years and years and years ago –
and nothing since then.

WILBOIS. The Academy is claiming the radio is a *French*
invention! And that Branly brought national honor to
France with it.

MARIE. You must be jesting.

WILBOIS. In addition – only a *small* portion of the credentials The Academy seeks for admittance concerns the significance and quality of the scientific work. There are equally important questions of – well – being a woman, Madame, to be honest – and having a foreign heritage – and non-Catholic beliefs – Even I – from Alsace-Lorraine? This I faced too from The Academy! It took three tries before they accepted me! "Not a true French accent! He is only half French – the other half? German! Too German!"

(silence)

So – the end of our conversation comes now, you agree?

(She nods slightly.)

You know, of course, in what high esteem I hold your work, Madame – and you! Bringing bad news to you? *Painful!* All the strength I could gather is what it took to come –

(beat)

MARIE. I understand –

(He glances at his timepiece.)

WILBOIS. So – I will be going home now for my dinner – Put this from your thoughts? And remember – please? I – so *many* of us are in awe of your work – your courage – your strength –

(He kisses her hand.)

Be well, Madame –

*(He starts out. **MARIE** sinks back in chair as **PAUL** enters, colliding with **WILBOIS**.)*

PAUL. I'm sorry! Professor Wilbois?

WILBOIS. *Ja, ja –*

*(**WILBOIS**, greatly upset, hurries off as **PAUL**, with articles, goes to **MARIE** in Parlor area.)*

PAUL. I brought what articles I could find –

> *(He looks at her.)*

> Your face is pale – what's wrong?

> *(silence)*

> You lost –

MARIE. By two votes – and a million same old reasons –

> *(She turns away.)*

PAUL. I'm so sorry! I –

MARIE. *(cutting in)* They'll never admit me! I've got to go back to the lab.

PAUL. But you're exhausted!

MARIE. If I isolate the radium into a solid metal – it will accredit me. They'll have to accept me in the Academy, then. No one will be able to take the discovery from me. There's no other alternative now!

PAUL. Let this damn career of yours alone for five minutes, will you? And let me love you?

> *(He kisses her, but she doesn't respond.)*

MARIE. Loving *me* is helping me do what I have to do –

> *(She starts reading article he's brought. Long silence. As **PAUL** paces around thinking something through. Then:)*

PAUL. We – we just found out – my mother – in – law? She must have surgery – in June –

MARIE. I'm sorry.

> *(She continues reading.)*

PAUL. Clotilde's going to care for her at home here in Paris – several months recuperation.

MARIE. I hope it goes well –

PAUL. We had already rented a summer villa in Normandy – with the Fournier family –

> *(**PAUL** paces more, then turns to her.)*

What if I decided to keep it? Children could be there with Madame Fournier – our Nanny, Jeanette – and Girard and I could come on weekends –

(*She continues reading.*)

MARIE. Sounds wonderful –

PAUL. There are – gardens – the beach – the guest cottage empty. Marie – come?

(**KATARINA** *enters.*)

KATARINA. Aunt Manya?

MARIE. Something wrong with the children?

KATARINA. Irène wants you to come read to her.

MARIE. Would you mind reading to her tonight, Katarina? I've a bad headache –

(**KATARINA** *exits, again lingering behind door, listening.*)

PAUL. And privacy. For God's sake, *privacy*! The guest cottage is secluded!

MARIE. Let me think about it – ?

(*She moves away. He follows her.*)

PAUL. *Mon Dieu*, we've never made love – not even *once!*

MARIE. Let me think about it?

PAUL. It'll be *our* summer, Marie! Please! Come!

(*He embraces and kisses her.*)

MARIE. All right – I'll come!

(*Cross fade. Normandy. June. Sunny, clear skies; a beautiful day at the villa. Flowers everywhere. Possibly teacart is used to hold flowers* **MARIE** *is replanting into pots.*)

KATARINA. *(offstage)* Aunt Manya? Aunt Manya? Aunt Manya – ?

(**KATARINA** *enters from Villa area in straw hat, summer dress, carrying shopping bag.*)

MARIE *(offstage)* Yes?

(**MARIE** *enters from cottage area in straw hat, flower at waist, summer skirt, blouse, sandals, carries gardening tools, begins clipping dead leaves from plant.*)

MARIE. Where are you going?

KATARINA. Village first – then the beach –

MARIE. So early?

KATARINA. I'm stopping by the dock – fishermen come in with their clams then –

MARIE. Clams?

KATARINA. For a French *bouillabaisse!* I'm going to make it for dinner!

MARIE. What a treat!

KATARINA. Jeanette's giving me the recipe – she's on the beach now with the children –

MARIE. Well, make sure Èvette's sunbonnet's on – and tell Irène I don't want her wandering into the waves.

(*beat*)

KATARINA. Irène says she wants to move into the cottage with you.

MARIE. But she's got such a lovely room in the villa...and I've told her I'll be distracted – writing into the night – starting at dawn –

(*beat*)

KATARINA. Come with us for the day at least?

MARIE. I've set myself a writing deadline. Tomorrow.

(**KATARINA** *lstarts down path, looks back at her.*)

KATARINA. Meet us at sunset then for a swim? Irène would be so happy –

MARIE. I'll go another time –

KATARINA. It would relax you, Aunt Manya.

MARIE. I <u>am</u> relaxed.

(**MARIE** *calling*)

Make sure Irène sees the sunset over the water –

KATARINA. *(Onstage but farther down path. Calling back.)* We'll be back for dinner –

MARIE. *(calling)* And...tell her to bring her Mama a beautiful shell – Wait – Maybe I'll –

KATARINA. *(stopping)* You'll come?

(silence)

MARIE. I – I'll start dinner – maybe – maybe – I'll – I'll bake a *gooseberry pie* –

(KATARINA exits towards village. MARIE looks after Her, wistfully. She begins digging in garden with spade.)

(PAUL enters, wearing city clothes, briefcase. He drops briefcase. She senses him. They look at each other, smile.)

(silence)

This week was eternity –

(He unbuttons, takes off vest, coming closer.)

PAUL. It's only five days since you left Paris –

(He rolls up sleeves.)

MARIE. Time is relative, Paul – remember?

(He smiles, they keep looking at each other.)

PAUL. An eternity for me too, Marie –

(She looks behind him, down the path.)

MARIE. Where are the Fourniers?

PAUL. They aren't coming.

MARIE. *At all?*

PAUL. Summer teaching position – last minute – for Girard.

MARIE. But weren't they paying a third – ?

PAUL. He gave me rent for us all for June –

(He looks around.)

Where is everyone?

MARIE. The beach –

(silence)

(He looks around more.)

PAUL. We're alone?

MARIE. 'Til dinner…

(PAUL moves to MARIE, embraces Her. He begins to undo Her blouse. She backs off.)

I'm filthy from gardening – mud – perspiration.

PAUL. You're beautiful!

MARIE. I'm not!

(He kisses her. She pulls back.)

What if someone comes?

PAUL. You just said no one's coming 'til dinner.

MARIE. That farm girl might come with our milk –

PAUL. *(chuckling)* No farm girl's coming with our milk!

MARIE. Or the mailman bicycling by –

PAUL. *(laughing more)* There's no mailman bicycling by!

(MARIE slides away, takes his hand.)

MARIE. Let's go inside – where it's cool and dark –

(KATARINA appears.)

KATARINA. Auntie Manya? I got wonderfully fresh –

PAUL. *(disappointed she's come) Bonjour,* Mademoiselle –

(He turns away.)

KATARINA. *Bonjour!* Where are the Fourniers?

MARIE. They aren't coming.

(silence)

(KATARINA looks from one to the other.)

KATARINA. It'll be just us then?

PAUL. Shouldn't you get the clams on ice?

KATARINA. The fisherman told me I'm to soak the clams in *salt water* – then ice. Then I'll go down to the beach with the girls – Oh – I stopped at the post office. For you, Aunt Marie. From Professor Wilbois.

*(She hands her letter, exits to villa. Angry, at **KATARINA**'s arrival, **PAUL**, picks up suitcase moves toward villa too.)*

PAUL. I may as well unpack –

*(He starts to exit. **MARIE** picks up envelope, pulls out a Newspaper page, skimming it.)*

MARIE. Paul – wait – Wilbois sent a letter published by *The London Times* from *Lord Kelvin* –

(reading)

"To the Editor: a reappraisal regarding the Curie's supposed discovery of radium is being seriously challenged by *my* theory. To be co-sponsored in Paris by The Sorbonne and St. Mary's Catholic Institute, where tentatively I shall be lecturer – a public debate of *both* mine and Madame Curie's theories is in the offing. Only procedural details to be agreed upon. Lord Kelvin."

PAUL. The letter in *The London Times* will certainly get him notoriety, but if he believed his theory had validity, he wouldn't have published it in a letter to the editor.

*(**MARIE** scrutinizes paper.)*

MARIE. And he doesn't state his affiliation at Glasgow, either – I think he's trying to come to St. Mary's teaching part time – then advance himself to a full time lecturer by inveigling *me* into a public debate.

PAUL. Write the paper immediately!

MARIE. I won't let him manipulate me!

(beat)

I must go back to the Lab – isolate the radium – immediately. And you must come with me. I think I can do it if you're beside me.

PAUL. I just got _here!_ I can't pick up now and leave! Neither can you! All the children are counting on us – Irène – Evette – and especially Christophe!

MARIE. There are wonderful things for him here without you – hiking – boating – swimming – the beach –

PAUL. Christophe wants me.

MARIE. Because you spoil him to death!

PAUL. I want to be a _good_ father to _my_ son – and I promised him the summer.

(She looks at him.)

MARIE. Then you must break your promise!

(silence)

PAUL. But I only know bare basics, Marie – I wouldn't be of any <u>real</u> help to you –

MARIE. You know more than you think you know!

PAUL. It's been years since I did _real_ experiments –

MARIE. I'll teach you –

PAUL. I don't think so! I-

MARIE. (*interrupting*) I'll make all decisions –

PAUL. I don't want to go!

MARIE. You _must_ support me!

PAUL. I said, I don't want to go! My house smells like a hospital – mother-in-law spread all over the parlor with her damn medicines? Clotilde shrieking at me?

MARIE. Kelvin is dangerous! He's striking out already. In no time, he could ruin Pierre's work of a _lifetime_ – and _mine!_

PAUL. September – September we'll go! Just a few weeks, really – Marie – it will be so wonderful _here_ with the children – the sea – your cottage –

*(**KATARINA** appears. They stop talking, move in different directions. **KATARINA** sees this.)*

KATARINA. I'm just going down to the children. Back soon. Maybe we could shuck clams together later.

(She runs out. PAUL *looks after her disdainfully.)*

PAUL. Is that girl going to be <u>everywhere</u> we are here?

MARIE. *(faint smile)* Probably.

PAUL. Like Paris?

MARIE. *(teasing)* Worse – it's summer – in the country – many, many acres – gardens to stroll in! Flowers to gather! A sprawling villa to roam through! *Freedom* for Katarina to be *anywhere – everywhere!*

(pause)

PAUL. I don't know – I don't know –

MARIE. Paul –

(pause)

PAUL. There's only one possible way –

MARIE. What?

*(*PAUL *has thought of this before.)*

PAUL. A *pied-à-terre.* To be with you – make love with you – every night – every day! I thought we'd have that here – but we won't –

MARIE. A *pied-à-terre?*

PAUL. *That's* the support *I would* need to go back!

MARIE. Paris has a million eyes and ears – and we'd both be coming and going from there!

PAUL. *(thinking it through)* We'll sign the lease – fictitious names! Never go together – one first – then the other – each with a separate key –

MARIE. I – I've never in my life imagined anything like this –

PAUL. <u>Imagine it</u>!

(She already has:)

MARIE. Well, it – it would have to have soft velvet furniture! And chiffon drapes!

PAUL. Yes?

MARIE. On huge windows – looking out to a garden –

PAUL. *(chuckling)* All right.

MARIE. Two rooms – one for work – one to live in – and walking distance to the lab –

PAUL. I'll find just the place.

MARIE. Then – maybe – maybe –

PAUL. Where we'd always have fresh roses?

MARIE. Yes – and good wine – sweet grapes – and crusty warm bread with soft brie?

PAUL. Of course –

MARIE. The way they did in a romantic novel I read once – when I was a girl –

PAUL. Whatever you want –

(Cross fade. The next week. Lights up on corner of Paris pied-à-terre *of the period. Summer. Living/dining space. Period chairs, table, lamp.)*

*(***MARIE** *with basket enters, stands transfixed – admiring, looking around, peaking into bedroom. She is very happy. She slides a note into a box on table.* **PAUL** *enters with bouquet.)*

PAUL. Marie!

MARIE. Paul!

(He sets bouquet down, goes to her, they embrace.)

I love it, Paul! Love it, love it, love it!

(She moves around room.)

Chiffon drapes – crocheted tablecloth – it's enchanted! –

PAUL. *(smiles)* Good –

(She sees roses.)

MARIE. Exactly what I want!

(She takes them arranging them in vase as he notices box. Takes note from it.)

PAUL. What's this?

(reading)

"My darling Paul – I embroidered flowers on this box when I was a girl in Poland – we'll keep our notes to each other in it – plans to meet – love letters – words too hard to say: I want to kiss your eyes – your cheeks your lips – lay with you in your arms – Your Marie"

(She turns away.)

Why don't you just tell me these things – what's wrong with you? *Je t'aime!* Can you understand what that means?

MARIE. I'm embarrassed –

(He turns her face to his.)

PAUL. Your eyes are beautiful. And your hair! And your skin! And your hands.

(He tries to take her hands to kiss them. She puts them behind her.)

Damn it! GIVE THEM TO ME!

(She does.)

Fissures – sores – burns – from radium you've touched – tubes of radium you've held in your hands!

(She has tears in her eyes, looking down. He takes her in his arms and kisses her hands. Looks at her fingers.)

I *love* your hands! Look what you've done with them!

Fingertips numb? You rub them against each other all the time – genius hands – discovering things to shake the world! Stop being shy! Stop being ashamed! Will you?

MARIE. Be patient? I've never ever done *anything* like this – never even been near a *pied-a-terre*.

(Silence. They kiss. Then she undoes his tie, unbuttons his vest. They go off toward bedroom.)

(Cross fade. Old, rickety lab.)

(**PAUL** *hurries in putting on labcoat. Begins setting equipment up on table as* **MARIE** *enters, donning Lab coat.*)

MARIE. Good morning!

PAUL. *Bonjour!*

(*She turns on the one light, takes notebook, comes to table.*)

MARIE. You came early. Setting up?

PAUL. Yes.

MARIE. Thank you, Paul – saves us time –

PAUL. Good.

MARIE. Double check though – before we start?

(*He looks at her.*)

PAUL. I've done it all.

(*But she puts on glasses, opens notebook, starts checking off items.*)

MARIE. Now – large beaker's secure on its stand – ? Flask's on its stand – higher than yesterday?

PAUL. Exactly what you asked for.

MARIE. Securely fastened?

(*She tests this.*)

PAUL. Tight as a drum.

MARIE. And you used that flask with the wire running through it –

PAUL. You think I don't know to use that flask? It's the core of the experiment, isn't it?

(*She doesn't hear him, involved in checking equipment.*)

MARIE. And the vials of mercury?

PAUL. Here – here –

(*She gets small glass rod.*)

MARIE. I'm going to tap the tube with this rod today – as the mercury drops down. That will make it drop faster –

PAUL. What's the difference?

MARIE. *All* the difference, I hope. Green radium chloride's in its bottle – ?

(She checks it, turns page of notebook.)

So – we're ready!

*(***PAUL*** *has looked away, distracted.)*

Paul?

(He turns back.)

PAUL. Oh – yes – of course

(She opens notebook, writing.)

MARIE. "August 12 – flask adjusted. Mercury to drop at <u>faster rate</u> – speed to be checked. Now – our first step: slowly – slowly – pour the green radium solution into the large beaker – two hundred milliliters exactly –

*(***PAUL*** *begins pouring liquid from bottle into beaker.)*

Slower – slower. Paul? Your hands are shaking. Put the bottle down before you start spilling.

(He puts down bottle.)

What's wrong?

(silence)

What?

PAUL. Last night – I –

MARIE. You what?

PAUL. I – I thought I saw Raymond in the street and it was midnight. After we left each other –

MARIE. Midnight? Clotilde's brother? He lives across the city!

PAUL. But what if it *was* him?

(beat)

MARIE. Raymond's only in your mind. Squelch it, Paul and pour –

(He nods, pours. She watches.)

Stop.

(He stops.)

One milliliter more – your hands are shaking – put the bottle down.

(He does.)

PAUL. I'm sorry.

MARIE. I can't waste a drop! It's all the radium I have in this world!

(silence)

PAUL. I said I'm sorry, Marie – but what if I really *did* see him?

MARIE. Pour the liquid into the beaker, will you? You must have done it a hundred times a year teaching –

PAUL. You think I stood around with the girls pouring radium into beakers? You need a senior chemist in here!

MARIE. I can barely afford <u>you</u>!

(Silence. Then:)

I'm sorry. That was stupid of me, and I didn't mean it

(He turns around.)

Can you finish pouring?

PAUL. I'll try.

*(**PAUL** finishes.)*

MARIE. Good! Next step's to activate the wire running through the tube. Turn the current on, please?

(He does, comes back beside her.)

Now – I'll pour the mercury down into the flask – tapping – drop by drop – over that activated wire – time it?

(She takes vial, pours mercury into flask, tapping flask with glass rod as he studies stop watch.)

Now – as it pours over the wire and slips down to the end of the tube – each drop should activate – and hang there a moment or two. Look – a drop's there already! Now – maybe – maybe the solution will start bubbling?

(beat)

PAUL. Nothing's bubbled, Marie.

(She's crestfallen.)

MARIE. The radium must separate from the chlorine and gravitate to the mercury drop –

PAUL. But it hasn't! The mercury sank to the bottom of the beaker! Nothing happened <u>again</u>!

(She looks back in beaker, tapping tube again.)

MARIE. Look – another drop!

(They're watching beaker.)

(beat)

PAUL. <u>Sunk</u>! *No bubbles! No radium pulled to the mercury*! We've tried this experiment three hundred times, Marie. Four hundred!

(He stops his watch. She writes in her notebook.)

MARIE. "First and second run-throughs August 12 – negative results" –

(Angrily he grabs notebook, flipping pages faster and faster.)

PAUL. And – September 19th – 20th – four run-throughs, <u>negative</u> results. October 10 – four run-throughs – <u>negative</u> results. November 11th – December 10th – January – February – 10th – 11th – 12th – six run-throughs

– _negative_! March – April – May – June – July – August – nine more run-throughs – NEGATIVE. More mercury, less mercury – flask higher, lower" – _nothing makes a difference_! Can we just stop early this _one day_ at least? We'll go on tomorrow! It's hot as hell in here!

(He throws down book. She looks sharply at him, staring him down.)

MARIE. We stop when I can think of no alternatives!

(silence between them)

Maybe – maybe if I tap even faster – so the mercury drops and...IT'S BUBBLING!! Chlorine evaporating – radium drawing to the mercury – mixing with it! _An amalgam_! Now – we vaporize the mercury – then only the Metal Radium will be left...

If we can only boil the mercury away now! Paul? Light the Bunsen burner. And don't tell me you don't know how to light a Bunsen burner!

(They both laugh. He lights the burner.)

Low temperature –

(He does this. MARIE _staring at flask as if a person.)_

Mercury? Please! Vaporize! What color would you be, Metal Radium? _If you are_ Metal Radium? Please! Be Metal Radium – and a beautiful color?

(Silence as she stares, transfixed. Then:)

VAPORIZED!!

(He looks.)

PAUL. But nothing's left! We've failed again!

(He turns off burner. She looks.)

MARIE. _Something was left_ – Tiny – white – shiny flakes – like bits of diamonds – THAT'S METAL RADIUM!

(They fall into each other's arms, looking into beaker.)

PAUL. But the flakes – some of them are starting to turn black –

MARIE. Trivial – from nitrogen in the air –

(She stares at flakes.)

PAUL. Maybe Wilbois is around to see it?

(PAUL exits. MARIE, embracing beaker, talking to beaker as if her baby.)

MARIE. "We are going to *vaporize* Lord Kelvin forever"!

(Cross fade. Pied-à-terre. Fall.)

(MARIE enters with bouquet of Fall flowers and leaves, basket of food, wine. Church bell chimes. She looks out, lays the table. Chimes again. PAUL enters. She runs to him.)

MARIE. We said seven – I was starting to worry –

PAUL. About what?

MARIE. I don't know – it's getting dark – carriages – horses pulling wagons –

PAUL. I'm sorry.

MARIE. I'm fine now you've come.

(She lights lamp.)

MARIE. I've even got a surprise –

PAUL. What?

MARIE. My article on metal radium's to be published: *Le Journal Scientifique*! And – I'm to present it at a conference in Bern!

PAUL. Marie!

(She smiles, lowers her head.)

(beat)

MARIE. This is both of ours! Let's celebrate?

(She pours wine.)

I bought a marvelous Bordeaux –

(She starts setting out food.)

Excellent brie – white grapes –

PAUL. I'm afraid I've eaten – just the wine –

(beat)

MARIE. *(extremely hurt)* But Saturday's *our* night for dinner
– and this is a special –

PAUL. I was at the lab this afternoon – Christophe bicycled
all the way from home with a surprise basket supper –
I couldn't disappoint him…

(pause)

*(**MARIE** gains control of her feelings.)*

MARIE. Clotilde's plan, I imagine?

PAUL. *(turning away)* Yes…

MARIE. Christophe bicycled off without you – in the dark?

PAUL. He's spent the night with the Dumas boy – close by.

MARIE. Surprising Clotilde allowed him the adventure –
she coddles him so.

(silence)

How're you doing with our class in your home?
Christophe's worn out *my* patience. I called him down
again yesterday.

*(Knock outside in hall. Both startled. **PAUL** signals
MARIE, who backs toward bedroom. He goes to door,
calling through it.)*

PAUL. Who is it?

VOICE. *(onstage)* Henri?

PAUL. You have the wrong flat.

*(Sound of fading footsteps. **PAUL**'s mood has changed.
He downs glass of wine. **MARIE** watches him a moment.)*

MARIE. What's wrong?

PAUL. Coming late like this – finding out the good news
about your paper – I – I didn't want to bring it up –

MARIE. What?

PAUL. I can't go on teaching for you – maybe one more
session –

MARIE. Over extended?

(He shrugs.)

(silence)

You're suddenly in such a mood.

(silence)

Paul?

(He turns around.)

PAUL. I – I think Clotilde may have gotten suspicious –

MARIE. *(greatly alarmed) Of us?*

PAUL. Yes.

*(**MARIE** looks sharply at him.)*

MARIE. Truly?

PAUL. Yes, That's why I felt I had to eat her supper with Christophe – ease everything –

MARIE. We've been *extremely* discrete here. The Sorbonne maybe? The lab – ?

PAUL. I don't know, but something.

(beat)

(She's growing more and more alarmed. Remains quiet, thinking it through.)

MARIE. I don't think we should be seen together – keep going to the lab – finish off the details – but only if Marcel is there – late afternoons. I'll go mornings – don't help me with my seminars. And stay away from The Sorbonne days I lecture –

PAUL. Clotilde wants me to quit *all* connections with *everything scientific* –

MARIE. She's always wanted that.

PAUL. But now her brother Raymond's found me a special industry position. Salary? A fortune! German company – new branch in Paris. Military equipment. They say Germany – all Europe – will be at war – soon!

MARIE. Your name's attached to the experiment. Your career's about to leap ahead *in science*! I'm opening up a new world with the proof of metal radium, Paul – can't you see that? And you'll be the linchpin.

PAUL. But I don't think –

MARIE. Get rid of Raymond nosing into your business! Get control of your wife!

PAUL. But she thinks *all* of science is a "Child's Game". She thinks –

MARIE. (*exasperated*) It must not matter *wha*t Clotilde thinks!

(*He turns away.*)

(*silence*)

Paul?

PAUL. Fine! Fine! I'll turn down the job –

(*church bell*)

MARIE. It's late –

(*She picks up basket, shawl.*)

Wait a few minutes before you leave? Walk east from the building – I'll go north – ?

(*She exits.* **PAUL** *downs last of wine, opens new bottle drinking from it, exiting.*)

(*Cross fade. Parlor. Late fall.*)

(**MARIE** *enters with briefcase from University. Doffs cape, sits.* **KATARINA**, *hearing her, enters parlor, takes envelope from pocket.*)

KATARINA. Aunt Manya? This letter came for you – from Sweden.

(**MARIE** *rises, stunned.*)

MARIE. Read it to me, Katya.

(**KATARINA** *opens letter.*)

KATARINA. (*reading*) "The Royal Academy of Sciences wishes to award the Nobel Prize for Chemistry to Madame Marie Sklodowska Curie, the first time this distinction will have been conferred upon a previous prizewinner. It will be given in recognition of advancement of chemistry and discovery and isolation of radium in a pure metallic state and for the study of the use of radium in treating cancer. In awarding this second Nobel Prize – the Academy wishes to acknowledge the breadth of importance we attach to Madame's recent discoveries. We invite you to be in attendance to accept your prize December 11, 1911. Derek Oleffsen. Secretary – The Swedish Royal Academy of Sciences."

MARIE. I just won a *second Nobel Prize?*

*(**KATARINA** embraces, kisses her.)*

KATARINA. *I knew*! *I just knew*! The minute you finished the experiment and published the findings.

MARIE. I – I need to sit down.

(She sits, in showck.)

KATARINA. No one's ever won *two* in science, have they?

MARIE. Not in anything – I don't think –

KATARINA. You look like you're in shock!

MARIE. *(realizing it)* I think I am –

KATARINA. Everyone must know now! EVERYONE!

MARIE. *Everyone's* in Brussels. There's a conference there.

KATARINA. Join it! Let them celebrate *you*!

MARIE. The work's taken such a toll. And I'd detest engaging in *chatter*. People – parties.

(pause)

But Einstein does present tomorrow. And he sent me his paper – inviting me to comment on a panel – then to go to dinner with him. I said no – but –

KATARINA. Go?

MARIE. Maybe – I need to think about it –

KATARINA. NO! You don't! It's settled!

(She exits.)

KATARINA. *(onstage)* I'm packing your clothes –

(beat)

MARIE. Then – then don't forget the papers from my desk?

PAUL. *(coming onstage, calling)* Madame?

*(**PAUL** enters.)*

Madame!

*(**MARIE** smiles. He goes to her.)*

Two Nobels?

MARIE. It's *your* victory, too!

(They embrace.)

(quietly)

I thought you'd left for Brussels –

PAUL. I wanted to congratulate you first.

MARIE. *(softly)* Einstein presents tomorrow – invited me to dinner – discussing his theories – how they link to my discovery – that the atom has components –

*(**KATARINA** enters.)*

KATARINA. Do you want your silk dress? Oh – Monsieur –

PAUL. Mademoiselle! *(with formality)* Madame – maybe you have a copy of that Hermann book? I'd like to borrow it for the conference –

MARIE. Katarina – would you mind looking for that book in my study? Hermann?

*(**KATARINA** nods, exits.)*

PAUL. *(whispering)* Einstein speaks *day after tomorrow*...you had the *preliminary* schedule. Sign in tomorrow night at the Conference?

(She looks questioningly at him.)

MARIE. *(whispering)* And tonight?

PAUL. *(nodding)* The *pied-à-terre*! Clotilde thinks I'm *in* Brussels – Katarina thinks you're *going* to Brussels. No one will know we're here in Paris!

*(**KATARINA** enters with small suitcase. They separate.)*

KATARINA. I couldn't find the book –

(She puts down suitcase, looking at them with suspicion.)

PAUL. *(to* **KATARINA***)* Thank you for looking, Mademoiselle –

(to **MARIE***)*

See you in Brussels, Mar – uh – Madame! – Mademoiselle?

(He leaves.)

(silence)

KATARINA. You're having an affair aren't you, Auntie Manya?

*(***MARIE*** turns away.)*

It's dangerous for you – he's a strict Catholic and married with *three* children!

(silence)

MARIE. *(still turned away, softly)* I love him, Katya – I can't go on without him now –

*(***MARIE*** picks up suitcase, exits parlor area. To outside* **KATARINA** *exits.)*

(Cross fade to pied-a-terre. Later that night.)

(Shadowy. **MARIE** *stops at entry. The door is open, room askew, disheveled, ransacked.)*

MARIE. OH! OHH!!

*(***MARIE*** looks around, backs up to open door. She hears sound from bedroom. Screams.)*

(hoarse whisper)

Paul – Is that you? Paul – ?

(silence)

*(***PAUL*** enters flat. She runs to him, clinging in embrace.)*

PAUL. *Mon Dieu!* We've been ransacked?

(He breaks from embrace, looking around.)

MARIE. We'd better report it right away –

PAUL. We can't report *a thing!*

(*They begin straightening.*)

MARIE. Then let's find the landlord –

PAUL. He'll phone the police! In a minute everyone will know where we are – who we are –

(*silence*)

(*They keep straightening.*)

MARIE. (*pensive, thinking*) Someone was looking for something in here –

(*She looks through articles on table, floor, then sees box of love letters under scarf. Grabs it, opens box.*)

All our love letters are gone!

PAUL. NO!

MARIE. They had a rampage in here – tore everything to pieces – then found what they came for! Clotilde thought you went to Brussels this morning. Does she think I went too?

PAUL. I told her you were home ill...so she wouldn't be suspicious about *anything* –

(**MARIE** *looking at him.*)

MARIE. She got someone to break in –

PAUL. How the hell would she know we had this place?

MARIE. Christophe.

PAUL. You insane?

MARIE. Remember that evening he brought you supper at the Lab? Then left on his bicycle while came here?

PAUL. What then?

MARIE. He waited – followed you –

PAUL. What are you implying?

MARIE. When I left here, Paul – I saw his red cap in the gutter –

PAUL. It's a common kind of cap! Don't make something evil out of him and Clotilde because they brought me supper that night! He's my son!

MARIE. He's *Clotilde's* boy! They both hate <u>me</u> – and she's jealous – suspicious of <u>us!</u>

PAUL. I can't believe Clotilde would persuade Christophe to –

MARIE. *(interrupting)* Who else could know where we were? Take love letters and *nothing else?*

PAUL. You think she has the letters?

MARIE. Don't you?

(beat)

PAUL. *(looking down)* If she does – she'll make a scandal.

MARIE. *(very alarmed) Scandal?*

PAUL. After teaching — a couple of days ago at my home – I gave the children a chocolate treat –

MARIE. Yes?

PAUL. Clotilde showed me a chocolate stain a child just made on her new chair. Then it started.

MARIE. What?

PAUL. She drinks – she got hysterical.

MARIE. About what?

PAUL. She sent the dish of candy flying at me across the room! Started screaming: "She's allowed to pick on *my* son — use *my* sitting room for her damn school – ruin *my* chair with chocolates? Is she allowed *my* husband's bed too? My brother Raymond can make the scandal of scandals in all the papers we own!"

(silence)

MARIE. We have to legitimize ourselves quickly, Paul. I can't be put in a position like this –

(He looks at her.)

PAUL. I can't divorce! Take what you want and go west – then I'll head south –

MARIE. You must divorce. Leave her – and the children.

(*silence*)

Permanently!

(*Cross fade to* **MARIE**'*s parlor.*)

(**KATARINA** *runs in with bundle of newspapers.*)

KATARINA. (*calling, frantic*) Aunt Manya? AUNT MANYA?

(**MARIE** *enters.*)

I got the papers like you said, but not one mention of your Nobel!

MARIE. What, then?

KATARINA. TERRIBLE HEADLINES!

(**KATARINA** *throws newspapers on floor, falls to knees reading paper after paper.*)

Le Figaro Journal: "Love Letters Found in *pied-à-terre*! Curie: Cruel!"

(*She picks up another paper.*)

L'Excelsior: "Student Langevin Deserts Christian Marriage for <u>Concubine Curie</u>*!*" *Les Temps*: "Madame Clothilde Langevin To Name Curie – <u>Co-respondent</u>!"

(**MARIE** *sinks into chair.*)

MARIE. They're – they're *all* her brother Raymond's papers –

KATARINA. You kept *love letters*? In a *pied-à-terre*?

MARIE. They stole them to do this!

(*Rock crashes window.* **KATARINA** *screams.*)

Shh! Get down!

(**MARIE** *and* **KATARINA** *sink to floor.*)

MARIE. Where are the children?

KATARINA. Safe – asleep – the back room –

(*Suddenly, rabble outside begins screaming. More rocks, crashes.*)

RABBLE. *(onstage)* "JEW WHORE PIG OUT!" "CRADLE ROBBER OUT!" "HOME WRECKER OUT!" "JEW WHORE! OUT! "DREYFUS JEW! OUT!"

*(**RABBLE** comes closer, continues under dialogue.)*

*(**MARIE** and **KATARINA** whisper through scene.)*

KATARINA. *(terrified)* How do they know we're Jews?

MARIE. For God's sake, we're not *Jews!*

(a beat)

KATARINA. Mama says you all grew up in the Jewish quarter – Freta Street – a synagogue across –

MARIE. Shhh!

*(**RABBLE** fades.)*

(silence)

KATARINA. They're gone?

MARIE. They'll be back –

(silence)

KATARINA. Our family got baptized – slid through –

MARIE. My sister's got a wonderful imagination.

(silence)

KATARINA. Mama went to our ancestors' villages! Our name Sklowdowska? On Jewish graves – records? Marked "J".

RABBLE. *(onstage)* "KILL POLISH PIG!" "FOREIGNERS OUT! "NOW! "DREYFUS JEW OUT!"

(another crash)

KATARINA. What if they kill us because we're Jews?

MARIE. Will you hush? We're not Jews!

RABBLE. *(onstage)* "JEW OUT! KILL THE JEW AND HER BASTARDS! OUT!"

*(**MARIE** runs away from window, dragging **KATARINA** along with her and pulling her to floor beside her.)*

*(**RABBLE** sounds fade.)*

(*silence*)

MARIE. (*whispering, thinking*) Forget the silly notions your mother's gotten into your head. We've got to get out of here – I can't be seen. You! Go lease us a hotel somewhere obscure: 2 rooms, 2 nights. Use a false name. I'll pack our bags, and the children's. Telegraph your mother: we're coming. Then go for train tickets to Warsaw – in 3 days. Use the cellar door and back alley.

(**KATARINA** *starts to exit.*)

(*beat*)

Wait! Paul – I think he'll be in the lab. Go tell him I need him badly –

KATARINA. You're playing right into his wife and her brother's hands!

MARIE. I have to have him with me!

KATARINA. You'll be ruined! And the children!

(*silence*)

MARIE. (*thinking, pacing*) I've got a standing invitation – the Warsaw Science Institute – they'll force me out of the Sorbonne now anyway –

KATARINA. Poland, then?

MARIE. I'd be Head of their Institute – I can get Paul an excellent position – wonderful opportunity for him! Hurry, Katya –

(**KATARINA** *exits.*)

MARIE. (*calling*) Tell Paul we all must leave immediately!

(*Cross fade to lab. Later that evening.*)

(**PAUL** *is packing.* **KATARINA** *enters.*)

PAUL. Katarina?

KATARINA. I must speak with you.

PAUL. You shouldn't have come.

(*He looks out windows.*)

KATARINA. Marie needs you. She's terrified. We're leaving our house tonight for a hotel.

PAUL. *A hotel?*

(She gives him paper with address.)

KATARINA. Here's the address – come tomorrow or late tonight if you can.

PAUL. *(looking at note)*

Marie and I must keep clear of each other – and everyone we know – and everywhere we go. I just came here to pack up –

KATARINA. They threw stones through our window – called her a Jewish Dreyfus whore! They threaten to kill her! And the children!

PAUL. Not many people are around here this time of day – go!

(He goes to door.)

KATARINA. She wants to go to Warsaw with you – make a *new* life together – she's been invited to head their Institute – and *you'll* have great opportunity –

PAUL. *"Opportunity?"* I've got three children!

KATARINA. But *Marie's* getting blamed! *HER career's* ripping to shreds! There are threats on <u>her</u> <u>life</u> – <u>her</u> children's!

PAUL. Threats'll be out on all our lives if I see her.

(silence)

KATARINA. *(enraged)* She was a renowned scientist in mourning – and *you? Teaching at three lower girls' schools!*

(He moves away from her.)

She was widowed! Free! *You* were the adulterer! And now you're <u>*walking away*</u>?

PAUL. You tell Marie – I'll contact her – when I can – that – that I'm trying to help us all out of this – in my own way – persuade Clotilde not to go to court – get Raymond to squelch the press – beyond that – I – I don't know —

KATARINA. I will tell *you* something, Monsieur Langevin: a different time is coming! Soon! One day *we all* will live completely equal! Stefan and I? A partnership with equal respect for each other – working side by side! A partnership! Not one up, the other down – because one's a man, the other a woman!

(She bursts out laughing at him.)

What a stupid way to live, Monsieur Langevin!

(Cross fade. Parlor. Later that night.)

(MARIE packing books. KATARINA enters, trying to slide unnoticed past MARIE.)

MARIE. Did you see Paul?

KATARINA. Yes.

MARIE. When is he coming?

KATARINA. He – he's afraid of being followed – at the moment – but he says: "Warsaw! A wonderful idea!" The two of you can plan everything there, he says – he'll join us –

(MARIE stops packing.)

MARIE. *Join us?*

KATARINA. Very – very soon. A – a week, two at the most. He'll contact you at my mother's –

(MARIE turns full attention to KATARINA, who keeps trying to leave room.)

He – he must do other things here, first —

(MARIE pushes chair from her path, ominously begins toward KATARINA, who keeps going, can't look at her.)

MARIE. What "other things"?

KATARINA. *(evasive)* Get Raymond – to squelch the scandal – get Clotilde – to withdraw divorce proceedings. No, I mean –

(MARIE advances on KATARINA, takes her arm.)

MARIE. Look at me!

(MARIE turns KATARINA around, forcing her to face her.)

You *dare* lie to me about *this*?

(KATARINA can't look at her. MARIE slaps KATARINA's face, then turns from her. KATARINA terrified.)

He will never come! It's finished!

(She pounds desk, throws books.)

OVER! OVER! OVER!

(several beats)

(She calms down, makes decision.)

We're going to Poland without him!

(turns away)

He couldn't take the leap – discovery – the unknown – *magic!*

(She sinks into chair. KATARINA tries to leave. An opened envelope slips from pocket to floor. She tries to retrieve it. MARIE sees.)

What's *that?*

KATARINA. Nothing –

(MARIE rises.)

MARIE. That's a telegram! And you *read* it?

(KATARINA tries to slide farther out of room, MARIE begins toward her.)

Where is it from?

KATARINA. Stockholm – trivial – something about seating arrangements – I – I'll take care of it – I –

(Terrified of MARIE, she stops.)

MARIE. Read it!

(Terrified of MARIE, KATARINA stops.)

KATARINA. (*with trepidation, stumbling over words*) "Dear Madame Curie – Because of the international publication of letters between you and Pierre Curie's student, Paul Langevin – and potential court proceedings which – which will name you co-respondent – The Committee – "

(**MARIE** *takes letter, continues reading.*)

MARIE. "The Committee asks you to cable you will not come to the Award Ceremony. Further, several distinguished Members of the Committee communicate that it would appreciated if you would inform us you do not wish to be awarded The Prize until such time as your name is cleared in the Courts. Had we known only a few hours before that you had been named co-respondent in a divorce proceeding, certain major Committee Members wish it known they would not have awarded you the Nobel Prize. Secretary of the Royal Academy, Derek Oleffsen."

(**MARIE** *sinks in chair.*)

Leave me, Katya –

(**KATARINA** *exits.* **MARIE** *grips the chair arms. After some moments she quietens, sees box of scientific journals in box nearby. Pulls them out, one by one, hugging them, rocking back and forth with them, caressing them as if they were her babies.*)

(*reading titles*)

"On the Chemical effects of Radium Rays," 1899 – "On the New Radioactive Substances and the Rays They Emit," 1900 – "On Induced Radioactivity Provoked by Radium Salts," 1901 – "On the Absolute Measure of Time," 1902 – "On the Emanation of Radium," 1903 – "On the –

(*She lays down journals with great care, as if babies.*)

All our work – done *here* – our careers – established *here* –

(moments pass)

Next – a new lab – an institute – <u>here</u>! Katya? Katya?

KATARINA. *(offstage)* Yes?

*(**KATARINA** enters with trepidation.)*

MARIE. Listen – I'm sorry – for striking you –

*(**KATARINA** sits, head bowed. **MARIE** softly touches **KATARINA**'s cheek. **KATARINA** slowly nods.)*

I want you to be with me – Katya? I need you —

KATARINA. Yes?

MARIE. First – write a letter for me to Nobel Secretary Oleffsen?

*(**KATARINA** slowly nods then slowly sits, takes pen, paper as **MARIE** gains great strength, dictating in strong, unshakeable voice.)*

"My dear Secretary Oleffsen: This is to inform you I will attend the ceremony in Stockholm. Furthermore, I would like to point out to those certain Major Members of this distinguished Committee – I cannot accept the principle that the value of scientific work should be influenced in any way – by a researcher's private life! Or gender! It has never occurred to me that a scientist's private life and gender is in any way connected to the value of that scientist's professional career, research – or contribution!"

(beat)

Let me sign it? *(She signs.)* "Madame Marie – Salomea – Sklodowska – Curie."

(pause)

We're staying in Paris –

(beat)

KATARINA. *(whispering)* You'll need me – 'til *March* – *April* – then?

(MARIE nods.)

I'll miss *another* year of school! That will end it for Stefan and me —

(MARIE looks at KATARINA, who's quietly crying, goes to her, softly caresses her cheek, kisses her.)

MARIE. It will be the beginning for you and Stefan.

KATARINA. How?

MARIE. I've decided I'm going to sponsor you through the Warsaw Conservatory!

(KATARINA whirls around, shocked.)

KATARINA. What?

MARIE. We'll see how far you can go...full-time – no money worries of any nature – only concentrating very hard on your music!

(MARIE smiles at her, rises, caresses her cheek.)

I'm expecting great things of you, you know!

(They kiss, then MARIE studies her, holding her at arm's length, brushing away KATARINA's tears.)

KATARINA. Auntie Manya – thank you – a million times!

(Cross fade. Nobel Prize ceremony in Sweden. Podium, baskets of flowers.)

(MARIE wearing brooch, formal gown enters.)

(round of applause)

(She holds Prize certificate, smiles, bows to audience.)

MARIE. *(confidently)* "The Swedish Academy of Science was kind enough to celebrate 'the birth of the science called radioactivity' by awarding the Nobel Prize for Physics to Pierre Curie, myself and Henri Becquerel for our *first* work in the field. Today – *pure, metal* radium – permanently lays the firm foundation of this new science of "radioactivity".

(*She steps from podium, at ease. Directly communicating with audience.*)

"In the beginning, Pierre Curie and I set out on a beautiful 'adventure of discovery'. We did not set out to cure cancer, nor to discern the true nature of the atom. Nevertheless, today, radium is the most useful, most powerful tool in radioactivity laboratories engaged in exploring possibilities for diagnosis and cure of cancer. I humbly accept the great honor of The Nobel Prize for my continuing research in this field. What great benefits there may be to mankind in the future if the atom is split, we do not know. – and so we now move forward into this new 20th Century – and into the chemistry – of the unknown – and the imponderable."

(*Cross fade: two years later. Sanitarium sunroom, Southern France. Sun streaming in windows. White wicker chairs.*)

(**MARIE**, *slightly gray, white shawl around her, sits, reading.* **PAUL** *enters.*)

PAUL. MARIE!

MARIE. (*smiling a little*) Sit?

PAUL. How lovely you look.

(*He sits, looking at her. She laughs, lightly.*)

MARIE. Always the flatterer! I've gotten a few gray hairs – I've been through major surgery –

PAUL. Well – as I said – you look lovely, Marie –

MARIE. I suppose a bit better than when I collapsed in Stockholm – I arrived here on a *stretcher* and they told me two years. It's almost that now – and I am getting stronger – The children come now – week-ends.

(*an awkward silence*)

Oh – and Katarina?

PAUL. Yes?

MARIE. She writes she's doing well at the conservatory – and is engaged to Stefan.

(They both smile.)

(another awkward silence)

Thank you for coming, Paul –

(Another silence sets in.)

I'm very grateful to you – and I wanted to tell you that –

PAUL. *Me?*

MARIE. Well – you saved us all. Quietened the scandal – I find barely a reference now in the Paris papers – and Wilbois writes it's never mentioned at the Sorbonne.

PAUL. It isn't –

(another awkward silence)

MARIE. *(smiling)* Paul, are you in the family business – or making German tanks?

PAUL. Neither. I've made a bargain –

MARIE. With the devil?

PAUL. Well – with Clotilde and her family.

(They both laugh.)

MARIE. What *kind* of "bargain"?

PAUL. That there would be nothing between you and me ever again – and I would go on with the marriage – give her another child if she wanted – if –

MARIE. *If?*

PAUL. Raymond squelched all the scandal in his papers – *and* agreed to <u>completely</u> support his mother – *and* give Clotilde an allowance from the estate – so I could go on at the Sorbonne and become a genuine Research Scientist. I just got a Fellowship for next term – based on my work with you.

(silence)

(**MARIE** *is very moved, close to tears. Subdues this, manages a restrained smile.*)

MARIE. I'm – I'm extremely proud of you...

(She sits back in chair composing herself, assuming a more formal posture.)

And I – I'll look forward to the time I'll be reading your articles, Paul –

(silence)

PAUL. Have they told you when you'll be leaving here?

MARIE. A few months, they say – I'm walking a mile a day now – but you know? Sometimes – I imagine I've got a *strange, new disease* the doctors don't recognize –

PAUL. Why on earth imagine *that?*

MARIE. A hunch – and you know – all my life I've gone on hunches. I know it's preposterous – but why – with *all* their doctors *and* their surgery and all their medications – why can't they truly diagnose what's wrong with me? I'll leave without the hint of a diagnosis – or – more importantly – a cure.

(silence)

PAUL. Finish recuperating in Paris then?

MARIE. I'm making plans for an Institute – for cancer research –

PAUL. A huge undertaking! When you first get back?

MARIE. There's urgency about it! I must start raising money immediately! I have invitations to go to America – and we all know that's where the money is!

(She laughs, but starts coughing more and more heavily. She coughs into hanky. He pours water from pitcher on table.)

Visiting time's nearly over. You'd better go – before some inane nurse comes rushing in scolding us – as though we were infants.

(beat)

MARIE. *(cont.)* Thank you for coming, Paul…

> *(She rises.)*

Oh – your hanky –

> *(Takes it from pocket, offering it to him.)*

PAUL. Keep it? For gambler's luck!

> *(She smiles, puts hanky back in pocket.)*

> *(a beat as they connect)*

> *(She then extends her hand. He looks at her, shakes her hand.)*

MARIE. Good-bye.

> *(He lingers a moment.)*

PAUL. Good – bye – "Madame" –

> *(Both recognize he's called her "Madame". She nods formally, he exits. She then holds hanky to her cheek, looking after him. Then turns from door toward the light streaming in the windows.)*

> *(blackout)*

END OF PLAY.

NOTE

Spanning a six year period (1907-1913.), *The Radiant* is suggested by true events and experiences in MarieCurie's life. Her husband, Pierre Curie, suffered shockingly painful back and leg bone problems, thought then to be early arthritis. Killed in a street accident, he left Marie a young widow with two small daughters to raise and support. She was offered – but turned down – a French government's Widow's Pension but acquired Pierre Curie's teaching appointment at the Sorbonne. She was rejected for membership by the most distinguished scientific organization in Europe: The French Academy of Science, although she held a Nobel Prize in Physics. Marie Curie then successfully isolated radium as a pure visible metal, having been challenged in a letter in The London Times by Lord Kelvin, another scientist, as to whether or not she and Pierre had actually discovered the new element of radium for which they'd won the first Nobel Prize. She received her second Nobel Prize in Chemistry, for isolating radium as a pure metal, having rejected several members of The Nobel Committee's wish that she forego the prize until she was cleared in a "high publicity" romantic scandal in which she was named "co – respondent". Though "whitewashed" by all concerned at the time, her affair with Paul Langevin, Pierre's student, almost ruined Curie's career and literally nearly killed her. He was a young, Catholic, married man with children. Though she and her family denied it, presumably because of the stigma of anti – Semitism on the rise in France since the Dreyfus case, there were proofs she was of Jewish heritage. Following acceptance of her second Nobel Prize, she broke down physically and mentally with strange, undiagnosed symptoms in what was then called "exhaustion", and was in and out of hospitals and sanitariums much of the remainder of her life, though she actively participated in WWI, taking medical classes, then going to the front to help doctors utilize X – Rays in surgery for soldiers. She also oversaw the building and administration of hospitals and institutions for cancer research and cure. Her daughter, Irène, became head of Marie's lab and won a Nobel Prize in 1934. Irène's husband, a physicist, also worked in the lab. Both became afflicted and died with the similar, strange illness Irène's father, Pierre, and mother, Marie, had suffered. The family's symptoms could not be diagnosed at the time, and Marie and her family were never cured. After WW II, Marie's malingering and finally fatal illness, and that of her family's, was generally understood to have been radiation sickness. Since Marie had discovered radium, it would have been impossible at the time for physicians to have diagnosed that she had died of her discovery.